SISTER OF THE BIRDS.

AND OTHER GYPSY TALES

Jerzy Ficowski

SISTER OF THE BIRDS
AND OTHER GYPSY TALES

translated by Lucia M. Borski

illustrations by Charles Mikolaycak

Abingdon—·—Nashville

Sister of the Birds and Other Gypsy Tales

Translation copyright © 1976 by Lucia M. Borski

These six tales were selected and translated from *Gałązka z drzewa słońca* by Jerzy Ficowski, published by Nasza Księgarnia, Warsaw, Poland, copyright © 1961 by Jerzy Ficowski.

Library of Congress Cataloging in Publication Data

Ficowski, Jerzy.
  Sister of the birds, and other gypsy tales.

  Translation from Gałązka z drzewa słońca.
  SUMMARY: Folklore collected from the gypsies of Poland which explains how birds know when to sing and why the cloud and sun are enemies.
  1. Tales, Gipsy. [1. Folklore, Gypsy. 2. Folklore—Poland] I. Mikolaycak, Charles. II. Title.
PZ8.1.F43Si   398.2'09438   76-11619

ISBN 0-687-38596-2

For my daughters
Christine
Magdalene
and Anna
          The Author

CONTENTS

SISTER OF THE BIRDS

SISTER OF THE BIRDS

THE GYPSIES CALLED HER THE Sister of the Birds. She summoned the birds when they were to sing. When she wanted the turtledoves to sing in the forest, only the turtledoves sang. When she wanted to listen to the cuckoos, the cuckoos only were heard. All she had to do was to throw a yellow kerchief over her shoulders for the whole forest to be filled with the trills of golden orioles. When she put on her pink apron, the chaffinches warbled in the trees; when she wore her russet skirt, the red-breast robins, chirping gaily, flocked to the woods. She had a dress also in dark dull stripes, which was her fortune-telling garment. She wore it as she crossed the woods on her way to the village, and the cuckoos did not stop their cuckoo calls, telling her what to say about the future to the curious ones.

The Sister of the Birds had an old grandfather, who had long been blind and completely sightless. He supported himself on a white stick cut from a birch branch and took pleasure in talking about colors. One day he heard the song of hundreds of chaffinches and golden orioles.

"Aha," said the grandfather, "the Sister of the Birds dressed beautifully today. She is approaching in her yellow kerchief and her pink apron."

He was not mistaken, for thus it was. The Sister of the Birds was not going to the village to tell fortunes, so she had put away her dark dull striped dress in a chest and dressed in her gay colors to bring out beautiful bird music for her grandfather.

Coming into the clearing just then, I heard the twitter and saw the Sister of the Birds and her grandfather sitting in front of their tent.

"Where are you going?" the Sister of the Birds questioned me.

"In front of me," I answered. "I have heard tell that whenever one goes in front of oneself, one always gets some place. And as you see, I came to this clearing and met you, although I did not know that you would be here. Had I not left my house, I would not have met anyone."

"That is true," said the Sister of the Birds. "But tell me, what are you looking for?"

"Tales," I replied. "So far I have not found a one. I gathered some berries and a few mushrooms, but did not come across a single tale."

"Stay with us," said the Sister of the Birds. "When we go wandering from forest to forest, you can come with us. I am sure we will come across many Gypsy tales, because at this time of the year the woods are full of them."

"Very well," I agreed. "I shall stay with you."

And so I did. Evening came upon us, and the Sister of the Birds and her grandfather went to sleep in the tent. The night being warm, I lay down on the grass under the open sky and looked at the stars. All of a sudden I noticed that the stars were disappearing from before my eyes one after the other, and the sky, which a moment before had been flecked with gold, was growing black. I climbed to the very top of a tall poplar tree, the better to see the stars and to find out the cause for their disappearance. As I was nearing the top of the tree, I saw the immense bird Czarana pecking stars from the heavens, just as the chickens peck millet. The bird Czarana sat at the very top of a tall tree and did not sing, but squeaked like a broken branch.

"Why do you eat stars and squeak?" I called to the bird. "Did the Sister of the Birds give you permission to do that?"

"I did not ask her," replied the bird Czarana. "It is night time; during the night the colors fade, and the Sister of the Birds has no power over anything. We, birds Czarana, have fed on stars and on women's milk from time immemorial. Do not bother me."

Having said this, the bird Czarana pecked the

remaining stars so that it grew completely dark. Fear overcame me, and I decided to make a fire to sit by until morning. I found a few small flints and in no time at all had a bright fire going to which I kept adding faggots and dry cones. It was still long before dawn when I found I had no more faggots or cones to feed the flames.

"What shall I do?" I spoke to myself. "In a moment it will be inky dark again."

I had hardly finished saying this when the ground stirred upward, as if a mole raised it on its back, and from under the ground emerged the monster Phuwusz.

I had never seen him before, I knew of him only from hearsay; he was more horrible to look at than I had imagined. He approached the fire and spoke to me.

"I know what worries you. You fear that the fire will go out, and you will remain without light during the starless night. Follow my advice. Take the blind grandfather's white birch stick and strike the fire with it seven times."

Having said this, Phuwusz disappeared under the ground, and I followed his advice. As I struck the fire, sparks flew upward to the sky, changing into stars. After the seventh stroke the sky was filled

with stars, while the grandfather's white stick had blackened until there was not a trace of white bark on it.

Soon the fire died, but the night was light, for the heavens were now studded with stars.

In the morning the grandfather, taking his stick into his hand, stood speechless with amazement. The scales had fallen from his eyes as the birch bark had disappeared from his stick, and his eyes were now able to see again all the colors in the world. His eyes were black as his stick blackened in the fire. The old man rejoiced, and the Sister of the Birds dressed in all the colors she had so that the forest filled with the warbling of the orioles, chaffinches, titmice, robins, turtledoves, cuckoos, nuthatches, rollers, flycatchers, and every sort of bird.

That day we packed up the tent and went on our way. During our walk I told the grandfather all that had happened the night before, and he related to me the history of the bird Czarana as other birds had told it to him.

I began to write down the Gypsy tales told me by the grandfather and the Sister of the Birds on pieces of birch bark with a bit of coal from the fire. Some of the tales were sung to them by the birds, some were whispered by the forest wind rustling in the

branches. Sometimes it happened that the grand-father would begin a tale but would fall asleep before finishing, so that the forest and the birds would bring it to an end. I hid the pieces of birch bark in the large hollow of an ancient oak.

So passed the summer and autumn. One morning when I awoke early, I saw the world covered by white snow that had fallen silently during the night. I grew sad for I thought that with the end of the summer the Gypsy tales would fall into a wintry slumber and be silenced until spring.

"You fret that the tales may be silenced," said the Sister of the Birds, "but you are mistaken. Presently I shall call the ravens, jackdaws, and rooks that will tell you tales the like of which you could not even dream about."

Having said that, the Sister of the Birds let down her long black hair that wrapped her like a black mantle. In a short while, cawing loudly, the jackdaws, rooks, and ravens came flying from all around. At first they sat in the snow, then scurried across the clearing, disappearing in the thicket.

"They've gone," I exclaimed. "They did not say a word. They just walked around and then left."

"Don't worry," the grandfather calmed me. "They told you everything they were supposed to

tell, but you did not notice it. Do you see the thousands of tracks of birds' feet in the snow? The one who reads the signs will learn the most beautiful tales. I can read the birds' tracks in the snow. If you wish, I can read to you what the ravens, rooks, and jackdaws have written."

The grandfather then read me a tale, and I wrote it down on a fresh piece of white birch bark. Soon I, too, learned the birds' letters, but I did not read as fast and smoothly as the grandfather, for I had to spell slowly, syllable by syllable, from juniper to juniper, from beginning to end. Then I wrote everything down on pieces of birch bark and hid them in the oak hollow.

One day early in the morning I heard the grandfather call me. At the tent I saw him blackening his white beard with coals from the fire, as a sign of mourning. He informed me with grief, "Sister of the Birds disappeared during the night— just now, when any day spring is to come and all the colorful birds are to return. Her tracks are still visible in the snow."

"Let us follow her tracks," I said.

I harnessed the horse, folded the tent, and we started out. We rode for three days and three nights. When on the fourth day the sun rose early in the

morning, we met the spring wind that melted the snow, and with it the tracks of the Sister of the Birds. After that, we did not know which way to continue. The grandfather grew sad although usually springtime made him joyous, even when he had been blind.

The sun was growing ever warmer. I pulled out the red featherbed from the wagon and hung it on an elm bough to air. During the long winter the feathers in the featherbed were all curled and frozen; now they could uncurl and take a fresh breath in the sun.

No sooner was the red featherbed hung, than from all sides of the woods red bullfinches flew and began telling me something, but I could not understand. The bullfinches then wrote with their feet on the remnants of the snow under a wide branchy juniper, "We come beside the red featherbed, because we, too, are red. You have called us at the last moment. Now that spring is approaching, we are ready to fly away. What is it you wish?"

"Please, tell me where the Sister of the Birds is and what has happened to her."

The bullfinches wrote that the Sister of the Birds had awakened in the middle of the night and had gone away following a white doe that held a

twittering sparrow in her mouth. The chase lasted for four days. On the fifth day the doe changed into a witch, the evil Urma, who imprisoned the Sister of the Birds in her castle tower.

"Follow us," said the bullfinches. "We are leaving very soon and shall fly toward the evil Urma's castle."

What a ride that was! The horse rode at full gallop behind the bullfinches flying above the woods to show us the way.

The castle of the evil Urma was surrounded by a high wall and wide water. As we came near the bullfinches flew off on their way. Quickly, I reached into the chest and pulled out the pink apron belonging to the Sister of the Birds. In a flash there came thousands of chaffinches, and every single one of them left me a pink feather. Then I took out the yellow kerchief, and a thousand yellow orioles came, each one bestowing upon me a yellow feather. Next I drew from the chest a brown gray cloth, and at the sight of that thousands of skylarks and ten thousands of sparrows flew up, and every one of them gave me a feather. Then I took from the chest a white sheet, and immediately a wild goose came, cackling loudly. He took all the feathers to the Sister of the Birds imprisoned in the castle tower.

For two days and two nights the Sister of the Birds sewed wings out of the feathers. On the third day she flew through the open window straight to us.

The birds spread the news throughout the forest. Soon Gypsy wagons began gathering, coming from all parts of the world to celebrate the deliverance of the Sister of the Birds. Many bonfires were lit, and old Gypsies began to tell tales. I wrote them down, one after another.

Then I recalled sadly the tales I had left in the hollow of the oak, but the Sister of the Birds let down her long black hair until it covered her like a cloak. The jackdaws came flying, and, upon learning what I needed, they flew away and soon brought me the tales from the hollow of the oak. Some pieces of the birch bark had been chewed by bark beetles. Here a tale had no ending; there, no beginning; and still another lacked the middle. I was forced to recreate them from memory, and when I remembered nothing, I guessed the missing part from non-memory.

Thus I collected into my bag Gyspy tales. I married the Sister of the Birds, and when our two daughters, Blackberry and Blueberry, were born I

decided to copy some of the tales and have them printed in this book for them and for all others who like Gypsy tales.

Turn the page.
There the tales begin.

THE MOTHER OF THE SUN

THE MOTHER OF THE SUN

MANY, MANY YEARS AGO when the Cloudking was very young, he lived in harmony with the Sunking. Those were good times! When the Sunking was resting after his long and tiring travels, the Cloudking left his palace and ordered his helpers to moisten the thirsty soil.

Never did it happen that the sun burned the earth when people begged for rain; nor did it happen that it rained when people wished for the sun.

On an afternoon one day, the Sunking met his friend the Cloudking and said to him, "Dear friend, I am exceedingly tired, for I had a lot to do. I was in a land drenched by a downpour during the night. I had to double and triple my efforts to dry the soil, otherwise the people would have had their crops ruined. Be so kind, do not disturb my work while I go to sleep."

"I am sorry," replied the Cloudking, "but I am just starting for that country now. You have labored in vain trying to dry it for I have decided to have the rain fall there for nine weeks without stop. Then the people there will know who I am."

"Why do you want to punish those poor people?" asked the Sunking.

"I shall tell you," the Cloudking replied. "There is

a monarch there who has a most beautiful daughter. I want her to be my wife, but the king, her father, opposes me, saying he has no daughter for a Cloudking. That is why I shall show his people who I am. I shall take all my followers—Rain, Wind, Lightning, Thunder, Hail, and Snow—and shall let them out together like hunting dogs upon that land to revenge my heart."

The Sunking spoke. "The poor people did not offend you. If you are vexed at their monarch, take revenge on him."

"I don't care," retorted the Cloudking. "Who can stop me?"

"I," exclaimed the Sunking.

"I would like to see it! I am curious to see it," said the Cloudking mockingly, and, turning on his heel, he departed.

The kind Sunking did not tarry. He sped as quickly as he could toward that land and reached it before the Cloudking and his helpers. When the Cloudking arrived, he could not attain his purpose, for the sun shone so brightly and warmly that the Cloudking's helpers had to flee so they would not burn.

The Cloudking was furious. He had to return to his abode with his followers burned and singed by

the fiery sun. From that time on he set out often from his castle at the summit of the highest mountains in the world for the land against which he had sworn vengeance. But the Sunking forestalled him every time, scattering his harmful band. The Cloudking's fury grew from day to day and from month to month. He pondered how to overcome the Sunking's might and power, and sought advice among his helpers.

Finally the Wind said to him, "You all know that our enemy the Sunking starts out at dawn as an infant. By midday he is a full-grown man, and in the evening he is a gray-haired old man who falls asleep on his mother's lap. If he could not sleep thus, he would not be reborn as an infant, but would remain a feeble old man. He would not be able to start on the morrow. We have to capture his mother, then her son cannot impede us."

Having listened to the Wind's advice, the rest of the Cloudking's helpers shouted and screamed with joy. Snow and Hail called, "Knarr! Klirr! That is the way!"

Lightning, running from corner to corner, screeched, "Kiskos! Kis! Kos! That will be fun! Kos! Koskis!"

Thunder boomed, "Boombaro! Boombaro! Boom! That will be well."

The Rain rippled, "Briszint! Szint! Szint! How shrewd you are, brother Wind."

After a moment the Cloudking spoke, "That is good advice. I shall try to seize the Sunking's mother."

Having said this, the Cloudking made his way toward the Sunking's home while that one was far away. On the way the Cloudking changed into a gray horse. Arriving at the golden house of the Sunking, the horse spoke to the Sunking's mother, who was sitting on the threshold.

"Good day to you, dear lady. I am Galehorse. Your son, the Sunking, sent me to take you to him as fast as possible. He is in the land drenched by waters and lacks strength to dry it. He would like to sleep on your lap for about an hour to renew his strength."

"My son had never requested that before," said the Sunking's mother. "But if he is really so weak, I want to hasten to help him as quickly as possible. I shall go with your help, if you will permit me to mount you."

That was all the Cloudking wanted. The Sunking's mother mounted the horse, and he flew as

fast as a gale to a large cave. There, changing back into the Cloudking, he locked up the mother of the Sunking.

Evening came. The Sunking was a weary old man. Coming home, he did not find his mother and could not go to sleep on her lap as he had been doing since the beginning of the world. He grew so weak, he could not move. On the morrow the sun did not rise, and the night did not cease, because the Sunking did not leave his home. It was dark everywhere. The Cloudking and all his helpers could do as they wished without a hindrance.

But that did not last long. A sharp and bright bolt of lightning flew off a cloud, striking the cave in which the Sunking's mother was imprisoned and split off a piece of the rock. The mother of the Sun caught the sharp edge of the lightning, and, as with the sharpest knife, she hollowed out a narrow opening in the wall of rock and squeezed free. She sped home to her son, taking his weary head on her lap. The Sunking fell asleep, and when he woke, he was an infant once again.

Next day he flew out the window and brightened the whole world. He drove the wicked Cloudking far away. The people in towns, villages, and forests rejoiced, singing and dancing in their gladness.

They thanked the Sun for its light for the darkness had lasted a full half-day, and people had begun to lose hope that they would ever again see a bright day.

Since that time there is no more harmony nor friendship between the Sunking and the Cloud-king, only enmity and quarreling, as between a dog and a cat or between fire and water.

WHERE BLOND PEOPLE CAME FROM

WHERE BLOND PEOPLE CAME FROM

LONG, LONG AGO THE GYPSY tribe Kukuja came to the foot of a high mountain to pitch their camp and stay the winter until spring. It was a good spot for the mountain protected them against the cold north winds.

The autumn was sunny and warm. While the sun shone warmly and the birds twittered gaily, the Gypsies sang and danced in front of their tents all day long and did not think of the winter. But one day in the twinkling of an eye, the sky grew cloudy, and the world turned pale and sad. The song stopped, although the dancers still tapped their feet, as if they had not noticed the clouds or the wind that flapped the canvas of their tents. Suddenly a blizzard whirled up, whitening the grass and the dancers' hair. Whipped by the wind and the snow coming from all sides, the Gypsies ran to their tents for shelter.

All at once they stopped in their tracks, as if rooted to the spot. Before the chief's tent stood a young maiden of unsurpassed beauty. Her face and hands were as white as the snow, and her hair glistened as gold burnished by the sun. Her eyes were as blue as early spring sky.

Speechless with amazement and fear, the Gypsies

surrounded her and looked at her with their black eyes wide open. She spoke in a whisper, "I am the daughter of the Fogking. I live far from here in the land of eternal snows. Word came to me that human beings know how to love, and that their love sometimes brings them happiness and sometimes pain. I do not know what happiness means; I do not know what is pain or what is love. I should very much like to feel the warmth of love, because I am cold through and through from the frost, and my heart is icy. Which one of you can tell me what is love?"

A handsome Gypsy youth called Korkoro, the Lonely One, stepping out of the throng, said to the light-haired maiden, "I fell in love with you the moment you appeared before my eyes. I loved you before you uttered a word. That which my heart feels is love, and as my love warms your heart, you will love me."

And Korkoro took Lighthair's hand into his own, but released it at once, for her hand was as cold as snow. Then he kissed Lighthair, but her face was like ice. Disregarding the coldness of her body, Korkoro led her to his tent, and on the morrow married the Queen of the Snows.

After a time the Gypsies noticed to their amaze-

ment that Lighthair had changed past recognition. Her face was no longer snowy white, but had turned a pinkish hue as the fog does at sunrise. Her hair shone no longer like gold, but now resembled the yellow blades of flax. She was even more beautiful for now she knew what love was.

Korkoro and Lighthair passed twenty years in happiness and gladness. Lighthair bore twenty children, and all of them resembled their mother. With every year the love between her and her husband Korkoro grew more deep and binding.

But the Fogking resented his daughter's long absence and decided to part her from her husband forever. One day when Korkoro set out on a journey to buy a brace of horses, the Fogking spread such thick, heavy fog that the man could not see even his own nose.

The Gypsy wandered through pathless regions as the treacherous fog led him farther and farther away from his tribe Kukuja. Finally, it brought him to the other end of the world from whence there was no return. There Korkoro had to remain.

Lighthair, still beautiful and young after twenty years, awaited her husband's return. One day her father came in a dense fog from his distant land and

told her what had befallen Korkoro and commanded her to return to his icy home.

Weeping bitterly, Lighthair spoke to the Gypsies, "My father orders me to return to him, and so I must leave you. Take care of my children, bring them up well, and love them the way I have come to love you."

She could say no more for her voice stuck in her throat and tears flowed from her eyes. At first her tears were hot, then lukewarm, then cold, and finally they turned to hail. Her pink cheeks grew paler and paler, and finally, as white as snow. Her flaxen hair, that used to dance in the breeze, grew stiff, heavy, and shone like burnished gold.

A thick cloud of fog rolled in enveloping Lighthair. The Gypsies, straining their eyes, saw her as she floated in the cloud, far, far above the summit of the mountain. They watched her until she was lost to sight.

In years to come her children married and had their own children and grandchildren and great-grandchildren, all of them light-haired.

Thus there came to be in the world light-haired, blond people, who continued to increase in numbers.

THE MAGIC BOX

THE MAGIC BOX

WHERE PINE WOODS MEET the beech forest there lived during the summer months a poor Gypsy couple. To have a roof over their heads on freezing days, they sought shelter during the winter in an old abandoned mill. But in the spring they returned to the pine woods and the beech forest to pitch their patched tent, frayed by winds.

There were only two of them, the Gypsy husband and wife. Although they had been married for seven winters and seven springs, seven summers and as many autumns, they had no children. They greatly desired a son.

One day the Gypsy woman went to the pine woods to collect cones. She gathered them from the ground and put them into a large kerchief, looking about her all the time. She saw a long row of ants walking one after another along paths, narrow as fingernails, carrying tiny white bundles in which slept their children, the little ants.

"Happy ants," sighed the Gypsy wife, continuing to collect the pine cones. Next, she watched a chaffinch in the juniper bush feeding black flies to her young ones. "Happy chaffinch," murmured the Gypsy woman, collecting more cones. Then she saw

a hedgehog leading her four babies for a walk. "Happy hedgehog," the Gypsy wife sighed again.

Throwing the kerchief full of cones over her shoulder, she returned to her tent where the pine woods meet the beech forest. Dropping the cones on the ground, she made a fire, for it had turned cold while she worked. The wind blew, a sad sigh came from the pine woods, and a rustle from the beech forest. The Gypsy woman sat down by the fire with her husband next to her.

"It is too bad that you have made such a large fire," said the Gypsy husband to his wife. "For just the two of us half of it would have been enough."

"Yes, that is true," agreed his wife. "But if we had children they would sit around the fire, and there would be enough warmth for all of them. Then it would not have been too bad to have thrown all the cones at once on the fire."

The cones made a large fire. The red flames flickered with golden wings, as if they wanted to fly away, but they could not. When the fire burnt itself out, the Gypsy husband and wife went to sleep inside the tent. They dreamed the same dream: a dream about a black-haired boy who was their son.

The Gypsy woman woke at dawn and went to the beech forest to gather beechnuts. She made

necklaces by stringing the beechnuts on hair from a horse's tail and sold them at fairs, for it was held that wearing the necklaces helped against pain in the joints. There were many beechnuts. The Gypsy woman had barely collected three fistfuls, when she saw a woman peering out from a hollow of an old beech tree.

It was Matuja, the soul of the tree. Leaning from the hollow, she spoke to the Gypsy woman, "Do not fear me for I am the soul of the beech tree, and I do not forbid you to gather the beechnuts. Tell me what you desire, and I shall fulfill it."

"O Beech Tree Soul," said the frightened Gypsy woman, "I would like to have a son."

"You shall have a son," Matuja told her. "Do as I tell you. When you go to the village to tell fortunes, look for a pumpkin that is as large and as round as the full moon. When you find one, cut it off the stalk and bring it to your tent. Then you must scoop out the seeds and pour it full of milk. Drink the milk, all of it, to the last drop. If you do that, you will bear a beautiful and happy boy. When he grows up, he will have to go into the world to seek the good fortune that is destined him. So that he does not wander empty-handed, here is a box made of beech wood—the box may be of use to him."

Handing the Gypsy woman a small wooden box, Matuja vanished. In a flash the hollow in the beech tree was grown over with bark.

The Gypsy woman was overjoyed and ran so fast to her tent where the pine woods meet the beech tree forest that she lost half the beechnuts she had gathered. Finding in the village a fat pumpkin, she scooped it out and filled it with goat milk, which she had gotten in exchange for a necklace against pains in the joints. She drank the milk to the last drop as she had been told by Matuja.

Awaiting the birth of her son, she was so lost in thought that she strung the beechnuts on her own hair. She noticed it only after the necklaces had broken and the nuts were scattered on the forest moss. She strung the nuts again, but in her absentmindedness she used cobweb threads which were still thinner and weaker than her own hair. The nuts scattered to all sides of the world, but the Gypsy woman did not grieve for great joy soon came to where the pine woods meet the beech tree forest—her Gypsy son was born.

The Gypsy husband and wife washed the little boy in the stream that had its source in the beech tree forest and flowed through the pine woods on to the sea far away. After bathing their baby, the

Gypsies named him Bachtalo, the Happy One.

From that time on the three of them warmed themselves by the fire in front of their tent—the man, the woman, and their son. There was enough warmth for each of them. The parents, although poor, were happy. But cold and hunger came as year followed year. The Gypsy wife did not always have enough clothing for her son during the cold winter months when the Gypsy family moved to the old, abandoned mill. Years went by, but Matuja's forecast was not fulfilled, only the Gypsy boy's name was Happy.

Early one morning, after twenty years had passed, Bachtalo left the tent, bade good-bye to his parents, and set out to seek his good fortune in the world. He took along the beech-wood box and a stick to chase away fierce dogs. He tramped the woods, choosing the winding paths. The friendly animals he came across in the thickets advised him of the best ways to go into the world. Since his earliest childhood Bachtalo had lived in friendship with the wild animals and understood the various tongues of the foxes, wolves, squirrels, and badgers. Bachtalo wandered through the forests, but nowhere could he find his good fortune although he

looked for it on the ground, in the hollows of the trees, and among the topmost branches.

One day an old badger told him to go south. To the south there lived the rich Forest King who promised to bestow good fortune on the one who would do for him something new that had never been done before.

"What is the good fortune?" asked Bachtalo.

"The king has promised to give the brave youth his daughter in marriage and half of his kingdom. I myself considered trying my luck, but I decided not to for I am old and my ears have turned completely gray. You, Bachtalo, are young," added the badger. "You should try. Perhaps you will be able to fulfill the king's wish and marry the princess. Go south."

"That I will. Thank you," said Bachtalo and went south. He crossed the pine woods and the beech forest, the fir wood and the maple forest, until he reached a spacious glade, the capital of the Forest King. In the center of the clearing stood a large red tent in which the king lived with his family.

Bachtalo entered the royal tent, saying, "I am the Gypsy Bachtalo. I come to you, Your Royal Highness, to fulfill your wish."

But the king's servants pushed the Gypsy out of

the tent, for the king was listening to the forest murmur and had no time for Bachtalo.

"Remember," said one of the servants, "that the king listens every day from five to seven to the forest rustling, and he is not to be disturbed. Come tomorrow earlier."

Bachtalo, leaving to find a resting place, thought that it would be well to look upon the princess before trying to see the king again.

Just then he noticed that the moon, as round and as large as a pumpkin, was rising over the forest. As Bachtalo passed near, it illuminated the lake in which the king's daughter was bathing. Bachtalo thought that she was beautiful, and was not mistaken, because she was truly lovely.

The following morning Bachtalo went to the king and said, "I heard, Your Royal Highness, that you will give your daughter in marriage to the one who will do something new that the world has not yet seen. I want to marry your daughter; tell me what I am to do."

The king's eyes flashed with anger upon hearing these words, and he shouted, "What can you be thinking of? You are asking me what to do? You know well enough that I will give my daughter to the one who is able to fashion a thing that has not

been done before. For your stupid question you shall go to prison."

Immediately the royal attendants caught the poor Gypsy and threw him into a dark dungeon under the roots of an old oak. They blocked the entrance with a big rock, and Bachtalo was left alone in darkness. It was cold underground because neither the sun nor the moon rose there. If an underground moon shone there, it must have been black for it could not be seen at all. Only moles came to Bachtalo to warm him with their soft furs. Bachtalo could not see them in the darkness, but he recognized their voices for he knew the moles' language.

How long Bachtalo sat in the dungeon is not known. But suddenly the darkness turned pale green, then grew quite bright, and Matuja appeared before the young man. Her long silvery hair resembled a running stream.

She whispered, and at first it seemed to Bachtalo that he heard the wind, then perhaps someone above him gathering dry twigs and cones. After a while Bachtalo began to understand Matuja's whispered words, "Do not be afraid and do not worry, Bachtalo. You will come out of the dungeon and marry the Forest King's daughter. I am Matuja, and

I promised your mother before you came into the world that you would be happy. I am come to keep my promise. You have with you the little beechwood box . . ."

"I have," said Bachtalo, squinting his eyes in the light, "but it is of no use to me. I collected bats' bones that bring fortune and put them in the box. I gathered four-leaf clovers and put them also in the box, but they dried up and turned to dust. I have not found good luck."

"Do not worry, Bachtalo," murmured Matuja. "Do you have a beech-wood stick?"

"I have," answered Bachtalo. "That was also of no use to me, for I came not across a single fierce dog that I had to chase away. But even if I had met such a dog and chased him, what good fortune would that have been?"

"Do not worry," Matuja calmed him. "Take a lock of my hair and cut if off."

As soon as Bachtalo obeyed her, she taught him further.

"Fasten some of the hairs to the box and the rest to the beech-wood stick. From now on the box will gladden or sadden the people according to your wish."

Taking the box into her hands, Matuja put it near

her lips and laughed softly into the opening. Then she wept and let a few tears fall into the box.

"Now, take the stick and move it back and forth against the box over my hair."

Bachtalo tried and from the box there floated into the world the most beautiful tones. While Bachtalo played and played, Matuja disappeared, and the dungeon again grew dark.

At first Bachtalo played slowly and mournfully. The blind moles listened to him and thought that autumn had come, that gray fog had spread over the earth and rusty leaves were falling into puddles. Next Bachtalo played lively and gaily, so that it seemed to grow warmer in the dungeon, and one could hear the flutter of wings and the twitter of thousands of birds.

All at once it turned light again. Bachtalo thought that Matuja had returned, bringing her brightness. But no! It was daylight. The Forest King had heard Bachtalo's playing, and he ordered his servants to remove the rock and bring the prisoner from the dungeon.

Bachtalo, standing before the king, said, "Look and listen, Your Royal Highness. Here is something that the world has not yet seen nor heard."

And Bachtalo played on his box. First he played a

sad song. The king wept mournfully, and from his tears grew many mushrooms, as after a heavy rain. Then Bachtalo played a gay tune. The king smiled. After the king, all his retinue, his family, and even the forest smiled. The princess smiled the happiest of all, and that very same day a wedding was arranged in the royal glade. Bachtalo brought his mother and his father from where the pine woods meet the beech forest, and everyone feasted and ate and made merry for three days. Bachtalo played the gayest of tunes. The king stopped listening to the forest murmur between five and seven because the music from the enchanted beech-wood box was more beautiful than the forest murmur.

Thus the violin came into the world.

THE ROSE AND THE VIOLINIST

THE ROSE AND THE VIOLINIST

ONCE THERE LIVED A KING and queen who lacked nothing, neither a golden roof over their heads nor food nor even treasures. At first they were gay and happy, but soon the queen grew sad and the king dejected because they had no children, although they desired them. The queen begged the river and the wind and the flame of fire to send her a baby, but all to no avail.

Finally the birds led the queen to an old woman knowledgeable in all kinds of magic—evil and good. When the queen asked her advice, the wise woman told her, "That is a difficult matter, my Queen. If you want a daughter I can help you. For a son I have no remedy. For a daughter, on a Thursday night just before twelve o'clock go alone to the cemetery and pluck the berries from an elder bush growing on a grave. Bring the berries home, and after three days, burn them. Then take a hair from a girl who is seven years, seven months, seven weeks, and seven days old. Put the hair with the ashes of the elder berries and boil them in a pot with bittersweet seeds. Eat the mixture, and you'll give birth to a daughter. Then when she grows up, give her to me to teach her magic."

"No," said the queen. "I shall not give her to you

for anything. Here you may have a hundred thalers for your advice, but nothing more.''

The sorceress took the thalers, but decided in her heart to punish the queen.

Returning to her palace, the queen did everything as the wise woman had directed her. The day after eating the potion advised by the wise woman, she gave birth to a gorgeous rose instead of a baby girl. The rose flew like a butterfly through the open window and out to a rosebush growing beneath it. The king ran with his servants to the garden wishing to pluck the rose, but he could not. Nobody was able to, so firmly did the rose attach herself to the stem and defend herself with sharp thorns.

Angered, the king hastened to the queen. ''Women as a rule give birth to children and not to roses,'' he said. ''You evidently are a sorceress, and I do not want to live with a sorceress nor even to dwell with her in the same land. I am banishing you from my kingdom. Begone!''

Before leaving the palace for exile in a distant land, the queen went to sit beside the rosebush, where she wept and kissed the rose. At the bottom of the flower a drop of dew glistened, and a very thin soft voice that was half sound and half perfume said, ''Do not weep, Mother. Drink the drop of dew

that glistens on my petals, and wherever you shall go you will find nourishment. Hunger will not come near you.''

With tears in her eyes, the queen swallowed the silvery droplet as her rose daughter wished, and went far away into the world. After wandering a long time, she came at last upon a forsaken badger's den deep in a forest. She spoke to herself, ''I shall live here. I do not wish to meet anyone, I do not want to see anybody, I prefer to stay here in the wilderness.''

She collected moss and grass to cushion the den so that she could live there. Every morning at the entrance to the den she found food and drink, and thus she never suffered hunger. But she had much sadness instead.

Although there was not a human being in the great forest, there was one who came to console and cheer the queen. That one was a bear. At first the bear came alone, but later on he was accompanied by his wife and his little cubs. They did not harm the queen, but jumped and danced in such a droll manner for her that often she could not help but laugh and, at least for a while, forget her sorrow. The birds sang to her their most beautiful songs, and flowers bloomed in colorful hues around

the den. Thus the queen lived in the forest for long months and years, knowing not what happened in her kingdom or how her daughter, the rose, fared.

Thus year followed year, and the rose bloomed in the royal garden without pause—in the spring and summer, the autumn and winter. Neither snow nor frost killed the red flower. The king came often to admire the beauty of the rose. But every time he approached, the rose would furl her petals, wither, and hang limply from the stem.

The king was grieved. One day as he stopped by the rose, he sighed sadly to himself, "If I only knew why the rose withers as soon as I come near . . ."

He heard a faint voice, saying, "You have banished my mother from the land, and now the poor dear must roam in the forest and live in an abandoned badger's den. If you were to repent and bring her back, I should cease withering at your approach and love you as a daughter should."

Upon hearing these words, the king sent his men to all sides of the world to search for the queen and bring her home. The men searched for her in the first side of the world and did not find her. They searched in the second side of the world and did not find her. They searched in the third side of the world and did not find her. They searched in the

fourth side and there found her. They had no need to search in the fifth side, but led her to the royal palace.

The king apologized to the queen, she forgave him, and a happier life began in the king's palace. But it was not a full happiness, because, instead of a lovely girl who would bring pleasure to the king and queen, a red rose bloomed for them. But she bloomed ever more lovely and no longer withered when the king was near.

With time, word of the magic rose, the royal daughter, spread far over the world. People came in throngs to see the unusual flower. There came noblemen and kings to bestow costly gifts on the rose. One king placed a golden mirror under the rosebush, thinking that the rose by looking in the mirror would be transformed instantly into a girl. But she did not cease to be a flower. Another king gave the rose a golden comb to comb her hair. But she did not cease to be a flower. The third king gave the rose a large box of cookies and candies. But she did not cease to be a flower. A flower need not look into a mirror nor eat sweets, nor has it hair to comb with a golden comb. The rose remained a flower as she had been, and did not change. The king sought advice from sorcerers, begged help from good and

evil Urmas, promising them a lavish reward for changing the rose into a girl. But nobody, not even the sorcerers' chief of chiefs, was able to perform it.

One day a young violinist came to the royal garden. He was a poor Gypsy, trying to earn his bread by playing on his violin. The king and the queen, looking out their window as the violinist entered the garden, heard him say, "Oh, what a marvelous rose! It would be a pity to pluck her, but I must kiss her at least!"

He kissed the rose and, sitting next to her on the grass, began to play such a doleful melody on his violin that the king and queen wept, and two glistening drops fell from the rose to the ground. Then the rose flew down from her stem and, changing into a maiden, embraced and kissed the Gypsy violinist.

"If anyone during the years had played for me like you did just now," she said, "I would have been turned into a girl long ago. But I am not sorry that I had to wait so long, for I have waited for you."

The king, the queen, and all the people in the land rejoiced as never before. The Gypsy violinist remained in the palace and later married the beautiful princess. To this very day he calls her his Rosebud.

ANDRUSZ WHO DISLIKED BEANS

ANDRUSZ WHO DISLIKED BEANS

ONCE ON A TIME THERE LIVED a poor Gypsy boy called Andrusz. He knew nothing about his father or his mother except that both had died long ago. He was an orphan cared for by no one. The Gypsies who fed him treated him poorly, giving him the hardest tasks to perform. They ordered him to bring dry wood from the distant forest, to curry the horses with moss, to grease the wagon axletree with butterfat mushrooms so that the horses would find their loads easier to pull, to scrub the blackened kettles with sand by the river, and even to pick fleas from the dogs' hairy coats. Andrusz fared ill among the Gypsies. They made him work as if he were a foundling or a settled farmhand rather than a Gypsy.

After his daily toil and sweat, he was given a bowl of beans to eat. Poor Andrusz! Although he was an orphan, still he was a Gypsy of one flesh and blood with the tribe, and a true Gypsy would never eat beans. Hungry as he was, Andrusz would not taste a single bean, but sat sighing over the bowl. His tears flowing into the bowl turned the beans so salty even the birds would not eat them, although Andrusz emptied the bowl in the birds' clearing every evening.

Poor Andrusz! He tramped the woods, feeding on berries and roots in order not to grow weak from hunger, because he had to work very hard day in and day out. He ate berries and roots and looked with envy at the other Gypsies who ate roasted partridges and hedgehogs.

One day Andrusz escaped from the Gypsies and set out into the world, thinking to himself that it might be better for him elsewhere. And so it was. He had not yet come to any place, but just being on the way, he was better off than he had been. Walking across the fields, he ate turnips and millet seeds. Crossing the meadows, he sipped sweet clover. Wending his way along the river banks, he ate fresh water carp caught on the sandy banks. Climbing the mountains, he hunted wild goats and roasted their meat over fire. He walked on boldly, straight ahead, without fear of anything. He avoided only the fields in which beans grew because the sight of beans made everything in the beautiful world look dismal.

Thus Andrusz wandered for seven days, until he came to a vast forest of huge trees and rocks. The sun still shone above the trees as Andrusz trudged into the forest.

The night came on, and the forest turned dark. Andrusz stopped and looked around not knowing what to do. Suddenly he saw two tiny lights shimmering through the trees and went toward them, thinking that perhaps they might be the lighted windows of a cottage. However, the nearer he came to the lights, the less he believed them to be from candles. They were neither yellow nor red as a flame, but greenish, resembling the glow of fireflies. Approaching quite near the lights, Andrusz saw that the gleam came from the eyes of a beautiful maid, standing as motionless in the forest clearing as if she were a young fir tree springing in its center. She motioned to him and spoke in a voice like the chirping of a cricket.

"Poor Andrusz! The Gypsies tormented you, as if you were a child of settled, not wandering Gypsies."

"How do you know?" asked Andrusz in fright.

"I know everything," the dazzling maiden told him. "I am the sorceress Keszalia. I know too that you are not the son of settled, but of wandering Gypsies. Not common ones either, but of the distinguished tribe Leila. Come with me."

"You will not harm me?" asked Andrusz.

"No," answered Keszalia. "You will serve me for

seven years, and if you fulfill your task well, you shall become rich. Then you will be able to take revenge on the Gypsies who ill-treated you."

Having spoken thus, Keszalia led him to her castle. Her eyes threw such bright light along the path that Andrusz was able to step around the holes and over protruding roots without straining his eyes. Keszalia's castle was built of gold and diamonds. Once inside she served Andrusz food and drink and then ordered him to carry out the mounds of sand that had collected in the chambers. He was to carry out the sand, not in a sack or box, but grain by grain. Having issued her order, the sorceress vanished.

Left alone, Andrusz wanted to cry. He spoke to himself, "So exquisite is Keszalia and yet so unkind."

He did not know that the most beautiful Keszalias are the worst of all.

"Evidently such is my lot," Andrusz thought, "that I cannot evade hard service anywhere, neither from people nor from sorcerers."

What was he to do? Sighing, he took to work. He carried out the sand grain by grain, trudging steadily day by day, and yet the piles of sand did not diminish. Thus almost seven years went by.

One day as Andrusz returned for another grain of sand, he saw that the mound was moving, and from it emerged the monster Phuwusz who had his dwelling under the ground. Phuwusz had dug his burrow under Keszalia's castle and thus made his way inside. He was Keszalia's great enemy and tried to harm her in every possible way. It was he who had brought all the sand into her castle and spread it throughout the rooms. Phuwusz came to the top of the sand pile and sat there looking like a large mole with a human head.

Having regarded Andrusz for a while, he said, "The seven years are almost up, your service with Keszalia is coming to an end, and it is impossible for you to remove all the sand. When Keszalia sees that you have not fulfilled your task as she ordered, she will banish you and give you a sackful of sand in punishment. When she comes here to banish you, stamp your foot three times and pronounce loudly the magic spell, cirkusz-pirkusz-phuwarusz. That is my advice to you."

Phuwusz then buried himself under the mound of sand in the chamber, and the mound became even larger. The pile of sand was higher than it had been seven years ago when Andrusz began his task.

In the evening Keszalia came. When she saw that the pile of sand had not diminished, but had grown larger, she blazed with anger.

"Begone," she shouted. "Take a sack of sand in payment, and let my green eyes see you no more."

She gave Andrusz a large, heavy sack of sand.

Andrusz took the sack of sand and was just about to leave, when he remembered Phuwusz' advice. He said loudly, "Cirkusz-pirkusz . . . ," but he had forgotten the third word of the charm.

The evil Keszalia was beside herself with anger. Her eyes shone with a gleam so fiery that the sand began to melt and change into glass. Andrusz' feet stuck in the molten glass, so that he was unable to budge. He called again, "Cirkusz-pirkusz-tralalusz."

Nothing came of it, for there was no "tralalusz" in the charm. Keszalia burned with such great anger that the castle shook. Poor Andrusz thought everything was lost because, even if he recalled the proper charm, he would not be able to stamp his foot for his boots were stuck in the molten sand. At that moment Phuwusz pushed his nose from under the sand, whispered, "Phuwarusz," and disappeared in his underground tunnel.

Andrusz, jumping out of the boots that he could not move and stamping his bare foot three times, called out loudly, "Cirkusz-pirkusz-phuwarusz!"

At that instant Keszalia turned gray, her face filled with wrinkles, and the green light in her eyes died out. She fell under the ground, and her castle vanished. Andrusz looked around and saw that he was standing in a clearing in a large forest, holding a sack of sand. But was it sand? Thanks to the magic spell, the sand in the sack had turned to gold.

Andrusz wanted to throw the sack over his shoulder and be on his way, but the sack was so heavy he could not lift it.

"What luck!" he exclaimed. "The Devil only knows what to do with it."

Instantly there was the Devil in front of him. Throwing the sack over his shoulder, the Devil said, "I shall help you, but first you must eat the bowl of beans I brought you. When you finish the beans, I shall carry your treasure wherever you wish."

Andrusz was terrified, not of the Devil, but of the beans. He ran, leaving behind the Devil and his sack of gold. He preferred to abandon his riches and remain a poor, homeless orphan rather than to eat the beans.

To this day he wanders over the world, eating turnips and millet seeds in the fields, sipping sweet juice from the clover, fishing for fat carp in the rivers, and hunting wild goats in the mountains. He is content for he needs nothing else.

GUIDE TO PRONUNCIATION OF GYPSY WORDS

Andrusz. *Ahn*-droosh

Bachtalo. Bahkh-*tah*-loh

Briszint. *Bree*-sheent

Cirkusz-pirkusz-phuwarusz.
Seer-koosh—*peer*-koosh—p-hoo-vah-*roosh*

Cirkusz-pirkusz-tralalusz.
Seer-koosh—*peer*-koosh—trah-lah-*loosh*

Czarana. Chah-*rah*-nah

Keszalia. Keh-*shah*-lyah

Korkoro. Kohr-*koh*-roh

Kukuja. Koo-*koo*-yah

Leila. Leh-*ee*-lah

Matuja. Mah-*too*-yah

Phuwusz. P-*hoo*-voosh

Urma. *Oor*-mah

THE GYPSIES CAME TO Europe from India, where it is thought they originated. They entered Poland from neighboring countries, perhaps as early as the fourteenth century, and found there less prejudice and persecution than in the countries from which they had fled.

Up to the Second World War in 1939, the Gypsies in Poland numbered between fourteen and twenty thousand. During the war they suffered great persecution, and many were put to death by the Nazis.

The Gypsies have preserved their spoken language, comprising many dialects. They have also learned the languages of the countries where they lived for long or short periods of time. A Polish traveler came across Polish-speaking Gypsies in Spain.

Since Gypsies do not have a written language, the beauty of their songs and folklore had to be collected and expressed by non-Gypsies. The poetry of the woman-poet Papusza, born in 1910, was translated into Polish by the author of these tales.

The Gypsies practiced the religion of the country in which they lived, retaining at the same time their ancient beliefs and customs. Being eternal wander-

ers, their chief occupations were as copper-, lock-, and blacksmiths, tinkers, fortune-tellers, and musicians.

In present-day Poland there are about thirty thousand Gyspies. The postwar government has been trying to settle them, giving the Gypsies land so they would become farmers or teaching them skills to become factory workers in cities, but, because of their deep-seated aversion to settled life, without much success. They prefer meager, scanty provisions, obtained by barter or occasional work, to a more affluent, settled mode of life. The Gypsy longing for open spaces, wandering, and freedom will not let them settle down.

JERZY FICOWSKI WAS BORN IN 1924 in Warsaw, Poland. He is a poet, eminent writer, and gypsiologist. He took part in the defense of Warsaw as a member of the Home Army. Taken prisoner by the Germans in September 1944, he was sent to the death camp at Oświęcim (Auschwitz). It is the translator's assumption that here he met Gypsies among his fellow prisoners, and his interest in them began.

Upon Mr. Ficowski's return to Warsaw at end of the war in 1945, he continued his interest in and studies of the Gypsies at the University of Warsaw, specializing in sociology and philosophy. During 1948 he lectured on the subject of the Gypsies in the University Department of Sociology.

Continuing his research, he lived and wandered with the Gypsies between 1948 and 1950. He learned their language, collected their folklore and songs, and compiled a Gypsy-Polish dictionary. He has translated into Polish the poetry of Papusza, the only Gypsy woman poet, was co-founder of the Gypsy Song and Dance Ensemble, and has written several books on Gypsies.

In 1949 he became a member of the Gypsy Lore Society, headquartered in Liverpool. His articles on

Gypsies have been published in the society's journal.

Lech Mróz, the reviewer of Mr. Ficowski's work *Cyganie na polskich drogach* (Gypsies along the Polish roads) in the *Journal of the Gypsy Lore Society* (volume 47, number 3-4, July–Oct. 1968), described him as a world-famous scholar of Gypsy lore. His research includes work in literature, archives, and direct field studies. He has a profound knowledge of the Gypsies' history, folklore, and problems. This is his first work to be published in a universally known language.

ABOUT THE TRANSLATOR

LUCIA M. BORSKI, WHO WAS born and grew up in Warsaw, Poland, developed her translating skills early. She attended a Russian school until she was twelve. As she read the folk and fairy tales she loved, she would translate to herself from Russian to Polish.

When a teen-ager Lucia Merecka Szczepanowicz came to the United States. Later, as a children's librarian and storyteller at the New York Public Library, she found few Polish tales available in English and began translating such stories herself. *Sister of the Birds and Other Gypsy Tales* is her eighth translation from Polish to be published.

Mrs. Borski has also worked as Assistant Head of the Slavic Languages Section of the Descriptive Cataloging Department of the Library of Congress.

ABOUT THE ARTIST

CHARLES MIKOLAYCAK'S lyric pencil drawings in *Sister of the Birds and Other Gypsy Tales* exemplify well his policy of careful study of costumes and background as a basis for his illustrations. Some of the research for this book he did in Hungary where many Gypsies live.

Charles Mikolaycak has won numerous illustration and design awards. *How the Hare Told the Truth About His Horse,* which he illustrated, was one of twenty books chosen to represent the United States at the 1972 Biennial of Illustrations in Bratislava, Czechoslovakia. His work has also been included in the Children's Book Council Showcase, the Chicago Book Clinic "Best of the Year Show," and the American Institute of Graphic Arts "50 Books of the Year" and "Children's Book Show."

Growing up in Scranton, Pennsylvania, Charles Mikolaycak earned a degree in Fine Arts from Pratt Institute. He and his wife Carole Kismaric, a free-lance author and picture editor, live in New York City.

Designer: Charles Mikolaycak

Illustrator: Charles Mikolaycak

The illustrations are small-scale pencil
drawings reproduced in halftone.

Typeface: Palatino—body
Korinna—Display

Manufacturer: Parthenon Press

Printing Process: Offset

Paper: 70# Mountie Matte

Endsheets: 65# Beckett Cover Stock—Black

Binding: Columbia Fictionette